HISTORY IN LITERATURE

THE STORY BEHIND...

ERICH MARIA REMARQUE'S
ALL QUIET ON THE WESTERN FRONT

Peter Gutiérrez

Heinemann
LIBRARY

www.heinemann.co.uk/library
Visit our website to find out more information about Heinemann Library books.

To order:
 Phone 44 (0) 1865 888066
 Send a fax to 44 (0) 1865 314091
 Visit the Heinemann Bookshop at www.heinemann.co.uk/library to browse our catalogue and order online.

First published in Great Britain by
Heinemann Library, Halley Court, Jordan Hill,
Oxford, OX2 8EJ, part of Harcourt
Education. Heinemann is a registered
trademark of Harcourt Education Ltd.

Editorial: Louise Galpine, Lucy Beevor,
and Rosie Gordon
Design: Richard Parker and Manhattan Design
Maps: International Mapping
Picture Research: Melissa Allison
and Elaine Willis
Production: Camilla Crask
Originated by Modern Age
Printed and bound in China by Leo Paper Group Ltd.

10 digit ISBN 0 431 08175 1
13 digit ISBN 978 0 431 08175 5

11 10 09 08 07
10 9 8 7 6 5 4 3 2 1

British Library Cataloguing in Publication Data
Gutierrez, Peter
   The story behind All quiet on the Western Front.
- (History in literature)
I.Title
   833.9'12

A full catalogue record for this book is available from
the British Library.

Every effort has been made to contact copyright
holders of any material reproduced in this book.
Any omissions will be rectified in subsequent
printings if notice is given to the publishers.

Acknowledgements
The publishers would like to thank the following
for permission to reproduce photographs/ quotes:
pp. 7, 21, 28, 32, 35, 37, 40, 47, akg-images;
pp. 20, 31, 46, akg-images / ullstein bild; **p. 4**,
Bridgeman Art Library; **p. 19**, Bridgeman Art
Library / (1153) The Mule Track, 1918, Nash,
Paul (1889-1946) / © Imperial War Museum,
London, UK; **pp. 24, 26**, Corbis; **p. 45**, Corbis/
Austrian Archive; **pp. 9, 14, 15, 41, 48, 22**, Cor-
bis/Bettmann; **pp. 29, 42**, Corbis/Hulton-Deutsch
Collection; **p. 39**, Corbis/John Springer Collection;
p. 11, Corbis/Michael Nicholson; **pp. 13, 34** Cor-
bis/Swim Ink 2, LLC; **p. 49**, Getty Images/AFP;
pp. 17, 33, 43, getty Images/Hulton Archive; **pp.
25, 30**, Illustrated London News/; **pp. 2, 10, 23**,
Popperfoto; **p. 16**, Rex Features/; **p. 44**, Rex Fea-
tures/Everett Collection; **p. 6**, The Fales Library,
New York University; **p. 12**, Topfoto; **p. 38**, Ullstein bild; **p. 27**, Wellcome Photo Library. **Cover**:
Magnum Photos/Herbert List; Cover background,
Photos.com. 1) All Quiet on the Western Front by
Erich Maria Remarque. "Im Westen Nichts Neues",
copyright 1928 by Ullstein A.G.; copyright renewed
© 1956 by Erich Maria Remarque. "All Quiet on
the Western Front", copyright 1929, 1930 by Little,
Brown and Company; Copyright renewed © 1957,
1958 by Erich Maria Remarque. 2) P19 - copyright
Siegfried Sassoon by kind permission of Mr George
Sassoon and Barbara Levy Literary Agency.

The publishers would like to thank Dr Thomas
Schneider for his assistance in the preparation of
this book.

**This book is dedicated to Belinda Loh, who made
the writing of it possible.**

Contents

Some words are shown in bold, **like this**. You can find out what they mean by looking in the glossary.

World War I

The 1920s were difficult in Germany. After World War I (1914–1918) ended, the nation was defeated, in debt, and at times without clear leadership. Unemployment was a major problem. Like many people, Erich Maria Remarque held a variety of jobs, working as a teacher, salesman, and journalist. He also wrote a novel based on his war experiences, *All Quiet on the Western Front*.

Some Germans blamed the war for their problems. What made Remarque different was that he did not blame Germany's leaders for losing World War I. Instead, his characters question why they are fighting at all. His book was not about amazing heroics, but was based on his own experiences as a teenage soldier.

World War I "kills" heroism

Armies had recruited young men like Remarque by appealing to their **patriotism**. Posters and songs stressed the glory of protecting one's homeland and performing heroic deeds. However, World War I was different from wars they had known before. It was the first war to make use of tanks, poison gas, and machine guns on a huge scale. It also featured **trench warfare**, in which fighting took place from deep ditches dug into the ground, designed to protect soldiers.

FREIWILLIGE ALLER WAFFEN sichert BERLIN
TRETET EIN IN DIE BRIGADE
REINHARD
WERBEBÜRO · 110 ABIT · NEUES KRIMINALGERICHT
TURMSTR 91

This German World War I recuitment poster shows the soldier as a heroic knight.

As a result, soldiers rarely saw their enemies close-up, even when killing them or being killed. Death was random, often a matter of being in the wrong place at the wrong time. Old ideas of heroism and bravery no longer seemed to apply. New ideas were needed, and Remarque's novel *All Quiet on the Western Front* helped provide them. Published in 1929, it struck a chord in readers – not only in Germany, where it sold a million copies in the first year, but also around the world. Readers sympathized with the soldiers Remarque described. These men survived bullets and **shells**, but something inside them had died.

Soldier as storyteller

Remarque's **narrator**, the German Paul Bäumer, records his boredom and his terror as a soldier. He sees friends die, and makes new ones, too. Wounded, Paul goes home where **civilian** life now seems strange to him. Throughout his story, the effects of war are presented through real-life details.

Remarque's novel is realistic and honest, and this has helped it to remain a bestseller and a grim reminder of the cost of war.

Life in the trenches was more than just dirty and cramped. Exploding shells could rain down at any moment. Packs of rats would swarm out of the mud. Unbroken sleep and fresh food were nearly impossible to find. Still, such conditions often bound soldiers together in friendship.

POPPIES

*"In Flanders fields the poppies grow
Between the crosses, row on row."*

Canadian John McCrae (1872–1918), a World War I doctor and soldier, is best known for a poem he wrote called "In Flanders Fields". Flanders, a region in Belgium, saw fierce fighting. Later, blood-red poppies bloomed in great numbers from the broken earth.

Remarque's peaceful childhood

In 1871, a German king named Wilhelm was crowned the first **kaiser**. This meant he was emperor of all the German lands. One of these was the powerful state of Prussia, which had just won territory from France in the Franco-Prussian War (1870–1871).

By 1898 there had been peace in Europe for a generation. That year, the author of *All Quiet on the Western Front*, Erich Paul Remark, was born. In 1921 he changed his name to "Erich Maria Remarque," but in a sense he kept his middle name by lending it to his best-known character.

At the beginning of the 1900s many Germans were wealthy, but not Remarque's family. Still, Erich managed to enjoy childhood activities such as fishing and butterfly collecting. In school he was called talented and gifted for his skill, not at writing, but at the piano. In fact, Remarque wanted to become a professional musician. That dream was later crushed, however, when his wrist was injured in battle.

Remarque (right), was the second youngest of four children. Here, he is pictured with his older sister Erna, and younger sister Elfriede. His brother, Theodor, died at the age of five. The Remarque children were brought up in a strict household.

By the early 20th century, Germany's railways linked small, peaceful towns like Ebernburg (above) to the country's mighty industrial centres.

Germany on the rise

Years of peace caused many Germans to have big dreams. Germany's industry and navy were the fastest growing in Europe and soon rivalled Britain's. Wilhelm II, the grandson of the first kaiser, was also the grandson of Britain's Queen Victoria. Therefore, to a boy growing up when Remarque did, there was no reason to expect a war between the two nations. In fact, in *All Quiet on the Western Front*, Paul relies on calm memories of childhood to comfort him while on sentry duty.

Now that it was an **empire**, Kaiser Wilhelm wanted Germany to have things that other empires had. The first of these was a powerful military force that could help rule German **colonies** around the world. Few Germans, however, expected his aggressive ideas to help trigger the biggest war in history.

Kaiser Wilhelm II (1859–1941)

Although some thought him devious, many Germans were fiercely loyal to Kaiser Wilhelm II. Even Remarque's fictional Paul Bäumer felt that he was not to blame for the start of World War I. In reality, Wilhelm wanted the war to continue even after some German politicians called for peace. In late 1918, two days before Germany officially surrendered, he gave up his throne and left the country.

Plans for peace . . .
or war?

German leaders believed France might try to take back the land it had lost in the Franco-Prussian War. They also worried it might get other nations to help. So, in 1879, Germany formed an **alliance** with the empire of **Austria-Hungary**, its neighbour in central Europe. France, however, soon made a similar agreement with Russia. Now Germany might have to fight on two fronts: east and west. To cope with this danger, Germany formed the secret "Schlieffen Plan", named after the general who designed it.

Due to Russia's great size, Germany thought that Russian troops would be slow to gather and become a real threat. In the meantime, Germany would focus on a swift invasion of France, after which the troops could help its weaker defences in the east. The key to the plan was surprise. Instead of attacking where French forces were strongest, the army would invade France through Belgium, which was **neutral**. Also, the plan was to be put into action not when fighting started, but as soon as foreign troops were even **mobilized**.

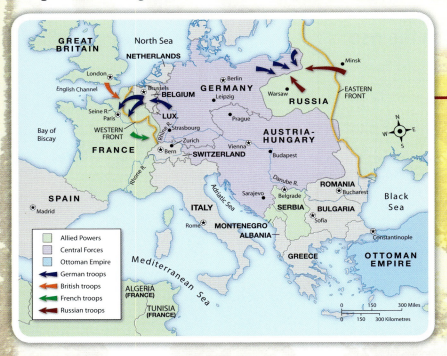

This map shows the directions from which rival armies attacked at the start of World War I.

How the War started

How did World War I actually start? In Remarque's novel, the soldiers do not seem quite sure. The character Albert compares the war to a fever: "No one in particular wants it, and then all at once there it is. We didn't want the war, the others say the same thing – and yet half the world is in it all the same."

The war started after the 1914 shooting of Archduke Franz Ferdinand, who was next in line for Austria-Hungary's throne. The killer was from Serbia, so Austria decided to punish the entire country. Russia had agreed to defend Serbia, and soon Russian troops were mobilized near Germany, which responded by declaring war.

At first the Schlieffen Plan worked. German troops marched through Belgium and into France. However, they were stopped at the Marne River valley, near Paris (see page 18). The possibility of a quick war was gone. Worse still, Germany had a new enemy! British troops arrived in response to Belgium's invasion. Britain's friendship with the United States also made German leaders concerned that US troops would also fight.

In 1914, many people in Britain thought their troops would be home by Christmas. After all, how long could the **Central Powers** of Germany and Austria hold out against the mighty **Allied Powers** of Britain, France, and Russia?

Valentine Fleming, a British army major and Member of Parliament who was killed on the Western **Front** in 1917, wrote in a letter home:

"*It's going to be a long war in spite of the fact that on both sides every single man wants it stopped at once.*"

Here, Franz Ferdinand's killer, Gavrilo Princip (second from right), is arrested.

Changed by war

When World War I finally ended, late in 1918, many people found it difficult to put it behind them. In fact, Remarque said his aim in *All Quiet on the Western Front* was "to awaken understanding for a generation that more than all others has found it difficult to work its way back from four years of death, struggle, and terror, to the peaceful fields of work and progress."

His character Paul has difficulty imagining doing anything normal with his life and suspects he is not the only one: "We agree that it's the same for everyone; not only for us here, but everywhere, for everyone who is our age . . . It is the common fate of our generation." Later he confesses, "I believe we are lost."

1919. Young soldiers of the King's Royal Rifle Corps, London, look forward to joining the Army of Occupation of Germany.

THE "LOST GENERATION"

After World War I, author Gertrude Stein used the term "Lost Generation" to describe the many American writers who settled in Europe. These included Ernest Hemingway, who was wounded by Austrian forces in Italy, and F. Scott Fitzgerald, who joined the army in 1917, but did not see any fighting. The writings of the Lost Generation whose members, Stein said, had "no respect for anything" were often bitter about the War, and US society in general. Still, the work of these writers was extremely popular in the United States in the 1920s, perhaps because so many Americans returned from Europe completely changed by their wartime experiences.

Weakened nations

Nations, like their soldiers, were also scarred by the war. There was the sense that countries had lost their most promising young men. Britain lost poets such as Rupert Brooke, Wilfred Owen, and Isaac Rosenberg, whose talents also included painting. The lives of those who did not fight were also changed. Like Paul's sister in *All Quiet on the Western Front*, many women saw their male relatives come home as strangers, if they returned at all.

Every war is terrible for its victims and the people who mourn them. So why did this particular war trigger such widespread feelings of disappointment and horror? Why was it known, even at the time, as the "Great War"?

British Poet Rupert Brooke (pictured in 1913), was killed in France during World War I.

Wilfred Owen (1893–1918)

Although Wilfred Owen wrote poems from an early age, only four of them were published while he lived. As a British officer, he fought at the Battle of the Somme (see page 18). In a hospital for mentally ill soldiers he met Siegfried Sassoon. Sassoon was a writer who guided Owen to create some of the finest poetry about World War I. Owen returned to battle and died a year later; a week before the War ended.

A new kind of war

"YOUR COUNTRY NEEDS YOU"

Many people were disillusioned by the time the war ended, although at first they had been very enthusiastic. When the war broke out, governments on both sides needed new recruits and public support, and had to convince people that they were fighting for the right reasons. As a result, World War I saw a heavier use of **propaganda** than any war before it. Propaganda is the spreading of information and ideas to influence what people think and do. Because some propaganda twists the truth or encourages people to hate or mistrust others, the term often has a negative meaning. Propaganda can take many forms, from songs making fun of the enemy, to pictures of soldiers looking healthy and heroic.

Lord Kitchener (1850–1916) was Britain's secretary of state for war at the beginning of World War I. This propaganda poster features his image.

Spreading unrealistic ideas

Remarque's readers probably remembered misleading propaganda in their own countries. One popular book had claimed that British soldiers benefited from their skill in football, a sport only recently introduced to Germany. The idea was that British troops had learned superior teamwork through playing football. A later pamphlet tried to reassure Americans who were about to send their young men to Europe to fight. It stated that the troops already on the Western Front were "fit" and "content" because they got regular meals and exercise.

German propaganda tried to win the support of people living under British rule in places such as Egypt and Ireland. Germany also tried to draw attention to **atrocities** committed by the French in their colonies in Africa. This strategy was partly a response to made-up stories, noted in *All Quiet on the Western Front*, about German atrocities. "But there are more lies told by the other side than by us", says Paul. "[Just] think of those pamphlets the prisoners have on them, where it says we eat Belgian children. The fellows who write that ought to go and hang themselves. They are the real culprits."

WAR OF WORDS

Before 1917, the possible US entry into the war was an important issue to both sides. German propaganda was aimed at German Americans and others who might oppose Britain. Meanwhile, British propaganda stressed Germany's sinking of ships, in which US civilians died. In 1916, President Woodrow Wilson was re-elected by promising peace, but the following year the United States declared war and started mobilizing troops. It then formed the Committee on Public Information, a propaganda agency that hired advertising professionals to promote the war.

The artist James Montgomery Flagg designed "Uncle Sam", a patriotic figure intended to represent every American, for this famous US army recruitment poster.

British soldiers guide each other, after being blinded by mustard gas on the Western Front.

Ghostly killer

Fritz Haber was a brilliant German chemist who won the 1918 Nobel Prize. During World War I he was in charge of a terrible new type of warfare.

In April 1915, British and French troops in Belgium saw a cloud move towards them on the wind. It was gas made from the chemical chlorine, and its effects were horrible. A few months later the British countered with their own attack. Although their gas was effective, some British troops were accidentally exposed to it. After that, gas was fired directly into enemy trenches. Gas masks quickly became common along the Western Front. In 1917, Haber introduced a deadlier weapon named **mustard gas**, after its smell. It was made from several chemicals, including chlorine. Contact with the skin produced blisters and damage to the lungs.

Paul eerily describes gas creeping along like a "big, soft jelly-fish", and remembers the gas patients in hospitals dying in "day-long suffocation". Remarque's description of the panicky putting-on of masks is similar to one in Wilfred Owen's poem "Dulce et Decorum Est". There, soldiers fit the "clumsy helmets just in time", while those not quick enough "drown" in the "thick green light" of the gas.

Monsters of sea and air

New weapons technology fuelled the enormous destruction in World War I. For example, although several countries had submarines, modern German **U-boats** sank so many ships that Britain's economy and food supply from overseas were seriously damaged for four years. This fact is more amazing given that Germany used only about 30 U-boats at any time!

Another new weapon of war was the aeroplane. Paul Bäumer expresses his hate for the **observation planes** that showed the enemy where to aim. In contrast, he comments that the "**battle planes** don't trouble us". Again, Remarque's writing reflected the average soldier's experience. Not until 1918 were large numbers of fighter planes used in battle zones.

Allied forces officers look at a captured German AV7 tank in France, 1917.

SURROUNDED BY DARKNESS AND MUD

Below the trenches were the dugouts where soldiers actually slept. As the name suggests, these were little more than holes in the ground. Enemy shells could easily make the shaky structures cave in, burying the soldiers inside in tons of mud.

There were no electric lights in the dugouts, so the soldiers were often in total darkness. They did not sleep on mattresses, but on wooden frames on which they could spread their blankets. There was a lack of hygiene and food was sometimes too spoiled to eat by the time it arrived at the front. Worse still, corpses could not always be moved away immediately.

Such conditions were ideal for rats. Unfortunately, Remarque did not invent the grim details in his novel, such as rats eating the precious food supply – and even dead bodies. Also, rats were not the only non-human enemy that troops had to deal with. Lice (insects that live in hair and clothing, and feed on blood) were a problem for all soldiers.

Nowhere to go

Modern technology created war machines that could take many lives at once. There were few ways to defend against these machines. If soldiers gathered to march in great numbers, they became tempting targets for powerful explosives. This situation led to armies remaining still and fighting at close quarters. In previous wars, an army might have charged into rifle fire and had a chance of taking an enemy's position. Now, however, the deadly effectiveness of machine guns often did not allow soldiers to get more than a few steps from their trenches. As a result, troops became stuck in fixed positions.

Army horses needed to wear gas masks too.

Even in their dugouts, World War I soldiers were at risk. Walls might cave in under enemy fire, and the filthy, unventilated conditions could cause disease. These French soldiers were photographed in about 1916.

Sergeant Merwin H. Silverthorn of the US Marines remembered:

You would take your blanket and ruffle it up, you see, and you didn't know if some rat had crawled in there or not. I mean these were great big field rats ... They weren't house mice. And the air down there didn't have ventilating systems on account of the gas danger ... Of course the bodies of the men hadn't been bathed. They didn't disrobe. They just lay down in their regular clothes. It was the foulest smelling air. Well, those were the dugouts.

Deadlocked armies

For most of World War I, no side had a clear advantage on the Western Front. Defeated troops would retreat a short distance, then retake the same land later. Sometimes an army would launch a major attack in the hope of ending the deadlock. In early 1916, the Germans attacked the French at Verdun. Yet, by the end of the year, the French regained their original positions. The only change was an additional 700,000 **casualties**.

Meanwhile, the British attacked near the Somme River in order to take the pressure off the French. They achieved this goal, but at a terrible price: 60,000 British troops were killed, injured, or taken prisoner on the first day alone. It is significant that Remarque made Kat, the most battle-hardened soldier of his novel, a **veteran** of the Somme.

This map shows the Western Front, and the locations and dates of some of the major battles of World War I.

Miles of scars

Powerful weapons forced each side into defensive positions in trenches. The trences often had three rows. The closest to the enemy, anywhere from 1.6 kilometres (1 mile) to 46 metres (50 yards) away, was the front-line trench. Behind it was the support trench, and behind that was the reserve trench. Communication trenches connected these rows. Sometimes these started in a distant town, getting deeper as they got closer to the battlefield. Going in the other direction there were tunnels for planting explosives beneath the enemy, dug by soldiers with mining experience. Today, those tunnels still weaken the Belgian houses built above them.

Trenches scarred the land, as did the repeated fighting that occurred between them in **No Man's Land**. Shells made deep craters, and entire forests were burned to the ground. Barbed wire, often electrified as Remarque describes, was placed to prevent grenade throwers from approaching the front-line trenches. In fact, Remarque had the dangerous job of going into No Man's Land at night to place new clusters of wire there.

Paul Nash, *The Mule Track* (1918). Nash shows us what the soldiers' view of World War I was from the trenches.

On April 25, 1916, poet Siegfried Sassoon wrote in his diary:

Looking across the parapet at the tangle of wire and the confusion of mine-craters and old fortifications, the prospect is not cheerful. Nothing grows; everything is there for destruction.

REMARQUE ON THE WESTERN FRONT

*One sign of deadlock was that Ypres, a Belgian town, saw battles in 1914, 1915, and 1917. Remarque fought in the final one, which featured tanks, poison gas, drenching rain, and tired troops – and became the source for many combat details in All Quiet on the Western Front. Remarque's friend Kranzbühler was hit by a British shell at Ypres. While still under fire, Remarque managed to drag him to safety. When Kranzbühler lost his leg, he became the basis for the character Kemmerich. Later, Remarque himself fell victim to an exploding shell. Besides the injury to his wrist, which cut short his musical career, the explosion left **shrapnel** in his neck. In the same blast, Remarque received a leg wound like Paul Bäumer. Also like his character, he was treated in a German hospital where doctors removed all the steel fragments from his body. None of Remarque's injuries significantly affected his health later in life.*

Being a soldier

An unusual number of **under age** soldiers volunteered to fight in World War I. Perhaps they were attracted by a sense of adventure and the chance to act like adults. Governments did not actively discourage them, and sometimes used propaganda that appealed to their youth. Both sides needed all the troops they could get. In Britain, the army did not make recruits prove their age with birth certificates until there was a public outcry. Recent research into government records has revealed that an incredible 250,000 soldiers were under age. Of those, it is thought that nearly half were killed or wounded.

Because they were desperate for fresh troops, the Allied and Central Powers armies allowed many under age boys to join the fight. This German soldier (pictured in 1916) is in his early teens.

At beginning of the 1900s, Germany had had a higher birth rate than the Allied countries. As a result, it had more troops than its enemies coming of age as the war continued. However, as in *All Quiet on the Western Front*, these soldiers were not well trained. Paul observes that the fresh troops are "boys . . . who cannot carry a pack, but merely know how to die", the type who "whimper softly for their mothers". Yet even this supply of boys ran out by the war's end. "Germany ought to be empty soon", remarks Kat in one of the final scenes.

Innocence sacrificed

Without a major war in their lifetimes, young soldiers were even less prepared for the reality of battle than their older **comrades**. Many held on to childish ideas about war, and often adults did little to teach them the truth. Some British propaganda even compared tank crews to football teams. Sadly, such ridiculous comparisons made sense to many under age soldiers. For them, war, like sport, offered a break from everyday boredom. This attitude can be found both in Rupert Brooke's poetry and his letters home, in which he wrote, "It's all great fun".

For Remarque, such innocence made the war all the more tragic. He often emphasizes his characters' youth. Müller still carries school books and dreams of exams. After new recruits arrive, many of whom are first-time shavers, Kat says, "Seen the infants?" When under attack, one settles under Paul's arm "like a child".

Of course, so many young soldiers led to broken-hearted parents across Europe. The scenes in *All Quiet on the Western Front* where Paul lies to his mother and to Kemmerich's mother to spare them the true horror of their sons' war show that Remarque understood the pain of the families left behind.

In uniform, these German soldiers may look like adults. But how old do you think the figure standing on the right is?

Some underage soldiers were more concerned about their parents' anger than the enemy's bullets. Tommy Gay, a 16-year-old British recruit, remembered:

I went home and told my mother I'd joined up. Well, she gave me such a beating ... I had no right to enlist, she told me, no right at all.

A fierce loyalty

Remarkably, many of the wounded soldiers wanted to return to battle as soon as they recovered. One US soldier wrote: "The magnet that drew me back to the front was the desire to see my friends again – to see what they were doing, to learn what they had done, to find out what had happened to so and so, to be glad that another friend was still alive and well."

Indeed, many soldiers felt that the only positive aspect of the war was the close friendships they formed. *All Quiet on the Western Front* touches on this theme again and again. Early on, Paul says that "the finest thing that arose out of the war" was **camaraderie**. A perfect example is the goose dinner Paul shares with Kat where he is moved to say that they feel "so intimate that we do not even speak".

WWI Allied troops celebrate the capture of a German canteen.

A unique bond

Paul's memories of camaraderie become bittersweet when he must say goodbye to his friends. These include Kropp, who loses a leg, and whom Paul says would have shot himself without his friends' company. Soon afterwards, Kat dies. This is Paul's saddest moment. However, Remarque made it clear that it was the constant possibility of such death that created deep bonds between the soldiers. "It is a great brotherhood", Paul writes, that arises out of "danger". He compares the soldiers' feelings of "desperate loyalty to one another" to those "of men condemned to death".

A wounded British soldier is helped by two German soldiers who had recently been captured by the Allies.

In real life, this camaraderie came at a price. A gap formed during the war between the soldiers and those who had not shared their experiences. These included women and men who had not fought. Remarque addressed this point by having Paul say "men will not understand us" – neither the "generation that grew up before us" nor "the generation that has grown up after us". Instead, they "will be strange to us and push us aside".

This seems like a very accurate prediction, but in fact Remarque wrote these words a decade after the war had ended, and was simply describing what he had seen.

BUILDING UPON FRIENDSHIP

Following the war, many veterans (ex-soldiers) formed groups in their cities and towns. These kept friendships alive and allowed the men to be useful in ways other than fighting. The US American Legion and the UK Royal British Legion are organizations of veterans who meet in local groups. Started immediately after World War I, the millions of members focus on caring for soldiers (and their families) who have fought for their country. The American Legion has even helped build hospitals and start a government bureau devoted to veterans.

Dangerous thoughts

Some of the most powerful scenes in *All Quiet on the Western Front* are those in which Paul encounters enemy soldiers. When guarding Russian prisoners, he notes that they look like Germans. He even brings them cakes made by his mother. Through such details, Remarque pointed out that the enemy is human, too, and deserves to be treated as such.

This was a risky theme to tackle, and Remarque knew it. When Paul reflects that a simple command from his country's leaders might turn enemies into friends, he is frightened to think such thoughts. If they were so close to being friends, why was nothing more done to avoid war? More importantly, if Frenchmen were not to be hated, wouldn't German soldiers lose part of their fighting spirit?

Here, a German soldier is being treated by British medical officers (1918).

"Forgive me, comrade"

Remarque showed that it is ridiculous to hate one's enemies when in so many ways they are not too different from one another. Most German soldiers, of course, would not have been aware of the similarities, because they had never met a Frenchman until being forced to kill one. This simple fact provides tremendous emotion when Paul is stuck in the shell hole with the French soldier he has stabbed. When the soldier dies, Paul feels that he has learned a great truth, and says to the dead body: "Forgive me, comrade; how could you be my enemy? If we threw away these rifles and this uniform you could be my brother . . ."

THE CHRISTMAS TRUCE

*An extraordinary thing happened on Christmas Day, 1914. Along the Western Front, there were unplanned **truces** that brought the fighting to a stop. As one British soldier wrote: "On Christmas morning we stuck up a board with 'A Merry Christmas' on it. The enemy had stuck up a similar one . . . Two of our men then threw their equipment off and jumped on the parapet with their hands above their heads."*

Eventually, several hundred soldiers from both sides were milling about in No Man's Land. Uneasily, they shook hands and together buried some of the dead. All of a sudden from the German lines came a tin can, and soon soldiers from both sides were playing with it as if it was a football. All the fighting was forgotten. Later a German soldier described how moving it was to see his friend's harmonica being played by a British soldier. Holiday songs were sung in both English and German. The British shared their plum pudding, and the Germans shared barrels of beer. In fact, the enemies shared just about everything with each other except their trenches.

Sadly, these amazing truces were soon stopped by the higher commands of both sides, and fighting began again.

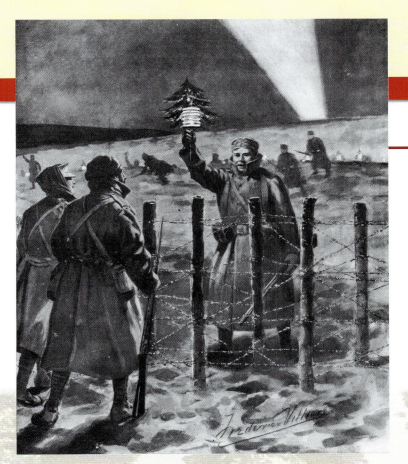

In this image from the *London Illustrated News*, a German soldier suggests a truce on Christmas Eve, 1914, by approaching British troops with a small Christmas tree.

Guilt and depression

In one of *All Quiet on the Western Front's* most powerful scenes. Paul visits different German dugouts. When he returns to each, he finds it destroyed, and his life spared only by "chance." **Psychologists** know that guilt about surviving terrible events that kill others is common in war. Remarque also knew that some of the soldiers who saw such horror were afterward unable to find meaning in life itself. They began to suffer from depression. This is a topic Paul addresses in the final pages of *All Quiet on the Western Front*.

Remarque was not the only author to tackle the **psychological** damage of war. Ernest Hemingway was an ambulance driver for the Red Cross in Italy, which fought on the side of the Allies. Later he joined the Italian army and was seriously

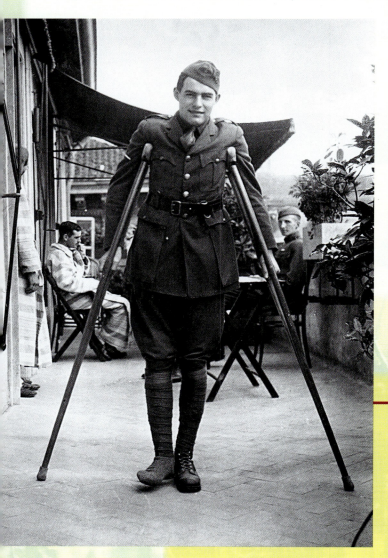

wounded. His novel *The Sun Also Rises* focuses on a wounded veteran who has trouble adjusting to post-war life. In *A Farewell to Arms*, a bestseller published the same year as Remarque's war novel, the central love affair is all the more moving because of the main character's emotional numbness after World War I.

Ernest Hemingway (here in his ambulance driver's uniform) was wounded in the line of duty in 1918. After this, he was given a medal for heroism.

Shell shock

Many soldiers were affected so strongly by the war's horrors that they were hospitalized. One of these was the British poet and writer Siegfried Sassoon who recovered and later returned to combat. Some say that he was the model for the character of Septimus Smith, the war veteran in *Mrs Dalloway*, a novel by Virginia Woolf. One of Britain's most celebrated 20th-century writers, Woolf portrayed Smith as a war-damaged writer unable to function in the 1920s. With a mental illness triggered by a friend's death in battle, Smith has wild mood swings and eventually commits suicide.

Shell shock was a condition suffered by huge numbers of soldiers in World War I. Symptoms included re-living **traumatic** events through nightmares and vivid memories, constant trembling or shaking, and being unable to keep quiet. Remarque included many references to shell shock even if he did not call it by name. "Two years of shells and bombs – a man won't peel that off as easily as a sock," remarks Kat.

In 1918, terrified faces like this one would have been seen in many army hospitals. This soldier has shell shock.

THE STRESS OF WAR

*What was once called shell shock (also termed "combat fatigue") is now commonly known as **post-traumatic stress disorder**. It is a psychological response to the extreme stress caused not only by war, but also by natural disasters and accidents. Sometimes those suffering from it feel like they are re-living events from the past. They can have intense anxiety about the original event, leading them to avoid things that bring back memories of it. They may seem emotionally numb or irritable, and have trouble sleeping.*

Loyalty to whom?

As in all wars, soldiers entered World War I wanting to protect their homeland. Like Remarque, however, many soldiers came to question the use of patriotic ideas by **insincere** people, as did the teacher Kantorek in *All Quiet on the Western Front*. As early as his training period, Paul finds that being loyal to his homeland can mean having to bury his own personality. However, Paul also describes his home with enormous love. The key to understanding Remarque's message here is in Kat's explanation of the difference between a person's "home country" and their "state". Home country (or homeland) is the place where people live with their fellow countrymen. "State", on the other hand, refers to the government that rules it. Remarque warned that patriotism and love of your homeland should not become blind loyalty to the government.

In 1914, Paris celebrated the 10th jubilee of the "Entente Cordial". King George V of Great Britain was present. The French were proud of their history and heritage, and had much to fight for in World War I.

German soldiers proudly
march off to war in 1914.
Their wives and families
sent them off as heroes.

Dangers of patriotism

Many real soldiers would have agreed
with Remarque's characters. One of
these was the British poet, Wilfred
Owen. His poem's title, "Dulce et
Decorum Est" refers to the sweet and
peaceful death that is said to belong
to those who die for their country.
Owen bluntly called this idea an "old
lie". He wanted his readers to know
that there was nothing peaceful about
most battlefield deaths.

Like Owen and other soldier-writers
such as Siegfried Sassoon, Remarque
did not attack patriotism itself.

Instead, he pointed out the danger of
using patriotism to mislead people.
As the character Kropp says, "[We]
are here to protect our fatherland.
And the French are over there to
protect their fatherland. Now, who's in
the right?"

Remarque warned of the danger of
patriotism blinding us to the painful
truth. As Paul says of people like
the teacher Kantorek: "We loved our
country as much as they . . . but
also we distinguished the false from
the true."

When his novel was published, Remarque exchanged letters with
British General Sir Ian Hamilton, who criticized it for its lack of
patriotism. Remarque responded to Hamilton like this:

*[All Quiet on the Western Front] presents the war as
seen [by] the front-line soldier . . . out of many separate
situations, out of minutes and hours, out of struggle,
fear, dirt, bravery, dire necessity, death and comradeship
. . . from which the word Patriotism is only seemingly
absent, because the simple soldier never spoke of it.*

Warfare breaks down

As World War I continued in deadlock year after year, causing countless numbers of casualties, some soldiers began to distrust their leaders. They felt that since the generals often lived many miles from the trenches, they did not understand or care about the typical soldier. In more recent times, historians have shown that these generals were not the lazy fools their soldiers sometimes thought them to be. They worked hard and often tried new ideas, but were **hampered** by everyone's lack of experience in fighting such a new kind of war.

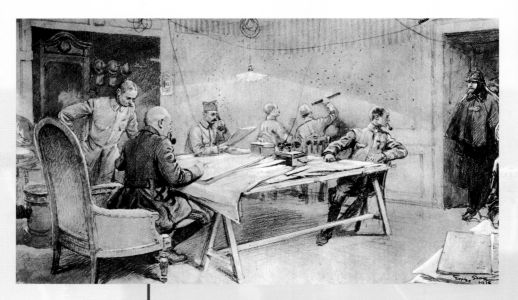

The artillery department of a French headquarters. Although it is near the Western Front, the high-ranking officers here enjoy luxury, and are in no danger.

Remarque showed the soldiers' resentment of their leadership in many scenes in *All Quiet on the Western Front*. Albert even suggests that only the politicians and generals of the two countries, armed with clubs, should go to war: "That would be much simpler and more just than this arrangement, where the wrong people do the fighting." In real life, some soldiers used this idea – that their leaders had no right to send them to meaningless deaths – as a reason to refuse to fight. In 1917, after one French attack failed miserably, large groups within that army stopped obeying their officers. Around 50 of these soldiers were executed, but the leaders who had ordered the disastrous attack were also replaced.

Power as poison

Remarque's criticism of authority went deeper than suggesting the leaders were not doing a good job. Time and again he presented the idea that when leaders get power, it actually changes them for the worse. The character Himmelstoss is the most extreme example of this in the novel. For him, being an officer means a chance to bully others. Another example of abuse of power occurs when Paul is on leave at home. Lost in his thoughts, he fails to salute a major, who then overreacts severely. When Paul mentions that he is on break from active fighting, this does not earn him respect.

Instead, he gets a lecture on the bad manners of soldiers from the front!

Remarque's characters also criticise the highest levels of leadership, claiming that these leaders benefit from war. As Kat comments about Kaiser Wilhelm, "every full-grown emperor requires at least one war, otherwise he wouldn't be famous". The soldiers' disappointment in the kaiser surfaces even after he appears in person to **review the troops**. "I imagined him to be bigger", comments Paul.

A German captain tries to rally navy recruits in Kiel, November 1918.

Not an advance

In his introduction to *All Quiet on the Western Front*, Remarque wrote that his book was not an adventure story because "death is not an adventure to those who stand face to face with it." In fact, both the war itself and Remarque's description of it helped change the popular idea of war as a heroic adventure. Instead, Remarque's characters show a quiet heroism. They admit their fear, but they do their duty anyway. When the novel actually mentions heroism, it does so in unexpected ways. "[We] were to be trained for heroism as though we were circus-ponies," says Paul. Later the characters call themselves heroes, not after a great battle, but after their revenge attack on Himmelstoss, a corporal in their own army!

Similarly, real-life heroes did not always act as expected. Siegfried Sassoon won a medal for his actions, but later threw it into a river. He hoped this would lead to a trial in which he could explain how soldiers were being misled. Instead, the military called him "temporarily insane" and placed him in a mental hospital. When he left hospital he returned to the front. Though he survived the war, he spent the rest of his life haunted by it.

This French soldier was shot after a court martial near Reims, France. On the post, he is described as a spy and a traitor to the fatherland.

Cowardice and desertion

In World War I, nations allowed their military to shoot **deserters**, who were considered cowards. Many had simply lost faith in their leaders. Others did not desert, but were reluctant to make "pointless" attacks. The French army alone found about 1,800 soldiers guilty of being cowards and executed a third of them. After the war, many of these dead men were officially found not guilty.

The British army shot about 350 soldiers for desertion. Some cases from World War I are still being investigated regarding troops fighting for Britain, such as those from Australia and New Zealand. It is thought that some of these soldiers, heroes in earlier battles, were actually suffering from shell shock later in this long war. Many of these soldiers wandered away from battle, and walked aimlessly behind their lines, not really in control of their actions, or with any clear plan. In contrast, Remarque's character Detering deserts the army in order to go home. However, this was clearly motivated by homesickness and not cowardice.

On 9 November, 1928, Sergeant Alvin C. York shook hands with the Mayor of New York, Jimmy Walker. York was given a ticker-tape parade for his war heroism.

Alvin York (1887–1964)

*The story of US infantryman Alvin York shows how close a hero can come to being thought of as a coward. Due to his religious beliefs he was a **conscientious objector**, and originally tried to avoid fighting in the war. What changed him into an international hero was not a sudden love of battle, but his closeness to his fellow soldiers. Realising that he could save the lives of friends, York killed 25 enemy soldiers in the capture of a German machine-gun post. In total 132 German prisoners were taken by York and seven other surviving Americans.*

Last moments

Because the sides were so evenly matched, World War I dragged on far longer than anyone expected. However, by the summer of 1918, the situation was changing and the truth became clear to many German soldiers. "Every man here knows that we are losing", writes Paul, explaining that "we have no more men and no more ammunition". Later he comments that the deaths at this point are "more bitter" because they happen "at the last moment", just as Paul's own death will. Here Remarque drew on the many real deaths that occurred so pointlessly at this stage of the war.

Paul says Germany's defeat is due to new and "overwhelming" forces. These fresh troops came mostly from the United States. Although the United States had declared war in 1917, it was not until 1918 that large numbers of troops – nearly two million by November – arrived on French soil. In contrast, a desperate Germany was running out of soldiers and was forced to send wounded soldiers like Paul back into combat as soon as they were healed.

JOIN THE
ARMY AIR SERVICE
BE AN AMERICAN EAGLE!
CONSULT YOUR LOCAL DRAFT BOARD. READ THE ILLUSTRATED BOOKLET AT ANY RECRUITING OFFICE, OR WRITE TO THE CHIEF SIGNAL OFFICER OF THE ARMY WASHINGTON, D.C.

This US recruitment poster was designed by Charles Livingstone Bull. How do you think it made people feel about the war?

Wilson's Fourteen Points

In early 1918, US President Woodrow Wilson proposed Fourteen Points to create a fair peace agreement for the winners and losers of the war. Throughout that year, Wilson's plan strengthened the arguments of those in the Central Powers who wanted to end the war. After several major attacks failed, Germany had no choice. On 11 November, its representatives signed an **armistice** with the Allies that ended the war. However, Allied bitterness toward their enemies, as well as secret agreements between nations, kept them from honouring most of Wilson's Fourteen Points. Allied commander, Ferdinand Foch (above, wearing long black coat) said, "It is not peace. It is an armistice for 20 years."

THE TREATY OF VERSAILLES

In 1919, Woodrow Wilson met with Britain's prime minister Lloyd George and other leaders in Versailles, a French city near Paris. There they worked on a long-term agreement, or treaty, between the war's two sides. The treaty was developed largely by France's prime minister Georges Clemenceau. Before World War I he had urged France to prepare itself against the threat of Germany, which is perhaps why people listened to him now. He insisted on disarming Germany and forcing it to make large payments, called **reparations**, *to pay for the cost of the war. German leaders reluctantly agreed to these terms.*

After the war

The end of World War I also meant the end of the German leadership that was in power when it started. Food was in short supply, and a generation of young German men seemed to have been wiped out for no clear reason. Also, many people wanted **democracy**, not an emperor. Several local disturbances, such as sailors refusing to obey orders, and workers going on strike, came together to form the German Revolution. There had been a similar revolution in Russia the year before, also caused partly by the war, and its ruler, the Tsar, had been executed. With his army too weak to help him, Kaiser Wilhelm decided to leave the country. The empire was dead, and a new National Assembly was elected in January 1919. It met the next month in the city of Weimar because the capital, Berlin, was considered unsafe.

Resentment towards the war was increasing. Many Germans felt they had been lied to, and were shamed by the harsh demands of the Treaty of Versailles. They had been told that Germany was defending itself against threats on two fronts, so they could not understand why it was blamed for Europe's devastation. Also, those who had planned the war, the Kaiser and his government, had left the country. So why should the average German be held responsible?

This map of Europe shows the new boundaries and countries in 1923.

These 1920s German children are allowed to play with money because it has become worthless.

Worthless money

In 1923, France invaded Germany's main industrial region, the Ruhr, to force the country to pay its reparations. Although many Germans thought these payments were unfair, they had a worse, economic reason for not paying. Unlike other countries, in World War I Germany had not raised taxes to pay for the costs of war. Instead, it just printed more money. Because there was so much of it, paper money was worth very little.

When money steadily loses value, forcing people to use more of it to buy the same things, it is called inflation. Germany's inflation continued to worsen after the war and became **hyperinflation**! Suddenly, everyday things cost many times more than they used to. Money was worth so little that some people burned it to keep warm. This situation created more enemies of the Weimar government within Germany.

THE ARTS IN 1920s GERMANY

*Although Remarque's characters seem to predict the chaos of the Weimar period, they could not have expected the new developments in the arts. In painting, Otto Dix, an ex-machine-gunner in the army, depicted war's horrors. Along with Max Beckmann, he helped launch a new phase of artistic **expressionism**. This style, which focused on feelings rather than showing things exactly as they appeared, was also used by filmmakers. Soon Germany's film industry became the most successful in Europe, with the work of directors Fritz Lang, Friedrich Murnau, and Georg Pabst receiving worldwide admiration. Metropolis, in particular, was a film that was said to have set a new standard in film making. The 1920s also saw authors Thomas Mann and Bertolt Brecht produce great literature. It was in this atmosphere that Remarque wrote his famous novel.*

"Remarque" is born

When he returned from World War I, Remarque taught for a while. He then held a series of jobs, including one as a journalist, that took him from his hometown Osnabrück to the cities of Hanover and Berlin. During this time he also wrote his first novel, *The Dream Room*, which was published in 1920. It got such poor reviews that Erich, still going by the surname, "Remark", decided to change his name. He used his late mother's name, "Maria" and the way his great-grandfather had spelled his name: "Remarque".

Remarque's first marriage to the dancer and journalist Ilse Jutta (Jeanne) Zambona lasted from 1925 until 1930. In 1927, he wrote *All Quiet on the Western Front,* although it was not published until late 1928. It appeared in **serialized** form in a newspaper. Right away it was a hit, as readers could hardly wait until the next issue to find out what happened to Paul and the rest of the characters. After lots of promotion by the publisher, when the novel came out in book form it was a bestseller.

ERICH MARIA REMARQUE

Im Westen nichts Neues

Remarques Buch ist das Denkmal unseres unbekannten Soldaten Von allen Toten geschrieben

Walter von Molo

This is the cover of the 1929 edition of *All Quiet on the Western Front.* The four large words are the title of Remarque's book in German: *In The West Nothing New.*

Worldwide popularity

Within weeks of its success in Germany, translations of *All Quiet on the Western Front* started to appear. Some estimates suggest that as many as 3.5 million copies sold within the first 15 months, in more than 20 different languages. Part of its appeal came from how Remarque used the voice of an ordinary soldier rather than using more sophisticated language. By doing so, he gave the impression that a real person was speaking. This viewpoint was fairly new, especially for war novels. As a result, Remarque received many letters from readers "who almost never [took] a book into their hands".

Soldiers also appreciated the novel. It showed them that they were not the only ones who had experienced fear, hopelessness, and even madness. Perhaps it even had a healing effect. In addition, Remarque's work gave people another way to honour the dead. Through its vast readership, the novel made sure that the public would not forget the sacrifices made by so many.

Lew Ayres starred as Paul Bäumer in the 1930 film version of *All Quiet on the Western Front*.

SILVER SCREEN SUCCESS

Millions more people became familiar with Paul Bäumer's story when the first film version of All Quiet on The Western Front was released in 1930. It went on to win the US Academy Award for Best Picture of that year. Though the German government later banned it from being shown in Germany, many people went across the border to Switzerland and the Netherlands in order to see it!

Praise from around the world

When *All Quiet on the Western Front* was published in Britain, the *Manchester Guardian* newspaper stated that it was "surely the greatest of all war novels". Praise elsewhere was almost as high, proving that the novel had apparently lost little of its power in translation from German into many other languages. In fact, its **universal** subject matter and simple language meant the book did not seem "foreign" to its readers. As one writer put it, ". . . that its author is a German is simply an accident. This book might have been done by a Russian, Frenchman, Englishman, or Italian".

The famous scientist Albert Einstein (centre) joined an anti-war demonstration in Berlin in 1923.

Upon its US publication, *All Quiet on the Western Front* was said to be a novel that helped readers understand the Lost Generation better. Its detailed description of the war itself was also appreciated. The influential Book of the Month Club compared *All Quiet on the Western Front* to Stephen Crane's classic novel of the US Civil War (1861–1865), *The Red Badge of Courage*. In it, Crane described the bloody war over slavery between US states in the North and South. Other novels had been written on the topic, but few from the viewpoint of an ordinary young soldier, the same kind of narrator Remarque was to use in the 1920s. Remarque also echoed many of Crane's themes, such as the foolishness of those who fight in wars hoping for personal glory or to be called heroes.

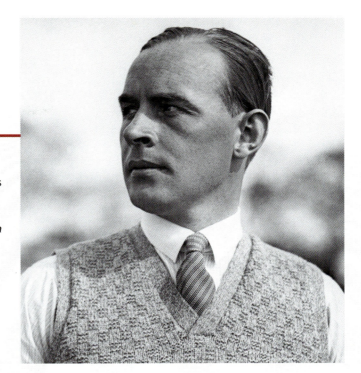

Remarque was an active, successful man during the years that followed the publication of *All Quiet on the Western Front*. Most of his novels were made into films, and he had several famous authors among his friends.

Stinging criticism

Some people were not happy with *All Quiet on the Western Front*. They thought it too simple, or not **literary** enough. Others disliked it because it seemed too critical of Germany. At one point, a military organization called the German Officers' League wrote a letter of protest to the Nobel Prize Committee after hearing a rumour that Remarque might be awarded its prize for literature.

Remarque himself tried to avoid political arguments about his novel "for it was not political . . . but human". He also reminded people that he was not a historian and could not examine the actual causes of the war or blame anyone for it specifically.

Here at last is the great war novel for which the world has been waiting ... Remarque speaks for a whole generation – that generation of the combatant nations whose life was destroyed in the springtime – even if it escaped actual death.

The *New York Times Book Review* on *All Quiet on the Western Front*, 2 June, 1929

War returns

During the time that the government was based at Weimar, many Germans looked for new kinds of political leaders. Some joined a new group called the **National Socialist Party**, whose members were called **Nazis**. Their leader was World War I veteran Adolf Hitler. Although he had been through many of the same horrible experiences as Remarque (such as fighting at Ypres), he came out of the war with very different ideas. In his writings, Remarque seemed to criticize those who falsely promoted the war, while Hitler cared only about blaming those responsible for Germany's defeat. In fact, Hitler could well have been a character in Remarque's next novel *The Road Back*. Often described as a sequel to *All Quiet on the Western Front*, it focuses on veterans returning from World War I and trying to make sense of society.

In 1923, Hitler led hundreds of armed Nazis to a beer hall in Munich where a local politician was appearing at a meeting. They took him captive and announced they were starting a new government. The police squashed Hitler's revolt, and killed 16 of his followers.

Crowds of Hitler Youth listen to Adolf Hitler speaking at a rally in the Nuremberg stadium in Germany, 1937.

Fascism is born

In prison, Hitler worked on his book *Mein Kampf* (My Struggle). In many ways, the ideas in it were the opposite of those in *All Quiet on the Western Front*. Instead of seeing the enemy as his brother, Hitler saw many of his fellow Germans as the enemy! He believed that "pure" Germans were superior to all races, and standing in the way of their greatness were Germany's minority groups, such as Jews.

Released after less than a year in prison, Hitler then focused on gaining power through elections. His plan was for Germany to build the largest army in the world, which it later did in the 1930s. Its purpose would be to increase German living space by conquering weaker nations. A similar political movement had taken control of Italy, where Benito Mussolini had ruled since 1922. Based on the Italian word for league, **fascism** promised to remake society through group strength and unity. Individuals were not important. Though fascism took hold in many countries, it was the alliance between fascist Germany and Italy that led directly to the next World War.

This woman is welding Messerschmitt tank parts in a German factory in 1941.

TRYING TO AVOID WORLD WAR II

In 1935, Italy invaded the African country of Ethiopia, and countries such as Britain and France did little to stop it. In fact, Britain allowed Italian troops to move through territory it controlled. A year earlier, Hitler had announced that Germany would rebuild its military, which was not allowed under the Treaty of Versailles. Again, however, little was done to stop Germany. In both these cases, powerful nations allowed fascist rulers to do what they wanted. Anything, it was thought, was better than fighting another war.

Cultural crackdown

After taking power in 1933, the Nazis tried to get rid of ideas and groups that they felt weakened Germany. For example, Fritz Haber, the German Jew who had pioneered the use of poison gas in World War I, became a victim of anti-Jewish policies. He was forced to resign from the Kaiser Wilhelm Institute for Physical Chemistry, which he had headed since 1911.

The Nazis branded Remarque a traitor because *All Quiet on the Western Front* was not completely patriotic. They thought his novels showed German weakness. Also, he showed soldiers as ordinary people rather than heroes.

The Nazis tried to hurt his reputation because they felt he was a Jewish supporter, which to them meant he was not a true German.

Paul Joseph Goebbels, who was in charge of Nazi propaganda, was behind this attack on Remarque. His goal was to replace Weimar **culture** with Nazi-approved art forms. As a result, the remarkable German film movement of the 1920s suddenly ended. After the Nazis turned that industry into a branch of propaganda, many filmmakers fled Germany for Hollywood.

GERMAN TALENT ABROAD

Cultural figures who left Germany to avoid Nazi rule included:
Thomas Mann (1875–1955), author
Nelly Sachs (1891–1970), poet
Albert Einstein (1879–1955), scientist
Walter Gropius (1883–1969), architect
Fritz Lang (1890–1976), film director
Alfred Döblin (1878–1957), author
Kurt Weill (1900–1950), composer
Max Beckmann (1884–1950), painter

In 1939, Remarque (right) was socializing with glamorous stars like singer Marlene Dietrich (centre).

In 1933, the Nazis burned books they thought were "un-German", including *All Quiet on the Western Front*.

Forced to flee

On the day before Hitler became Germany's leader in 1933, Remarque crossed the border back into Switzerland where he had been living since 1932. Here, the Nazis had little support. A few months later, he listened to reports on the radio as his work went up in flames. Along with the work of Hemingway and others, copies of *All Quiet on the Western Front* were burned in massive Nazi bonfires. Five years later the government officially declared that he was no longer a German.

To help his former wife, Jeanne, avoid life under the Nazis, Remarque remarried her in Switzerland. Then, like many leading German artists and scientists, he settled in the United States, far from the Nazis' grasp. Here, he and Jeanne lived apart until their second and final divorce in 1957.

However, Remarque did not fully escape the terror and tragedy that other Germans experienced under the Nazis. His sister Elfriede (see page 6), who had stayed in Germany, was accused of making negative remarks about Hitler's government. In 1943 she was executed.

45

Germany comes full circle

In 1939, only a decade after *All Quiet on the Western Front* reminded the world of the horrors of war, World War II began. After invading Poland, France, and other nations, Germany controlled much of Europe until its defeat in 1945. By that time, the war had grown to include fighting in places such as North Africa and Asia. In the Pacific Ocean the United States spent more than three years in a bloody struggle with Japan, which was on Germany's side. World War II is thought to have killed 25 million military personnel, in addition to 30 million civilians. Three quarters of the world's population, across 61 countries, were involved in World War II.

As in World War I, fighting on Western and Eastern Fronts proved costly for Germany, as did the late arrival of US troops in Europe. Remarque went on to write about German military aggression towards Russia in his 1954 novel *Time to Love and a Time to Die*. His only play, *Full Circle* (first performed in 1956), concerned the end of World War II in Berlin. From the title alone, you can get some idea of Remarque's view of German history in the 20th century: history had repeated itself.

Adolf Hitler visited Paris on 28 June, 1940. Paris was taken by the Germans on 14 June.

THE HOLOCAUST

*During World War II the Nazis were responsible for the **Holocaust**, in which millions of Jews and other people were murdered. Remarque dealt with this subject directly in Spark of Life. However, a section of All Quiet on the Western Front seem almost to predict parts of this horrific crime. While in the hospital, Paul meets a doctor who operates on soldiers' flat feet. Paul soon learns the operation is a "scientific stunt" that the doctor has been trying to master since 1914, sometimes breaking the same bones repeatedly and leaving his patients crippled. In his cruelty, this character resembles the Nazi doctors who later performed experiments on people during the Holocaust. Again, history seemed to be repeating itself.*

Another road back

After World War II, many of the mistakes that followed World War I were avoided. In fact, the victors even helped Germany to rebuild. However, the country was divided into East Germany and West Germany for more than four decades. In a sense, this division represented another difficult "road back" that Germany had to travel.

Remarque spent the remainder of his life in Switzerland, where he became a citizen in the 1930s, and in the United States, where he gained citizenship in the 1940s. He occasionally returned to Germany, but was sad and somewhat bitter about no longer being a "German". In 1958, he remarried, this time to American film star Paulette Goddard. He died in 1970 of heart failure.

Russian soldiers hoisted up their flag on the **Reichstag** in Berlin at the end of World War II. This is a reconstruction of the event.

World War I in the arts

The literature of World War I, including *All Quiet on the Western Front*, the writings of Siegfried Sassoon, and the poetry of Wilfred Owen, continues to touch readers decades later. In 1962, composer Benjamin Britten used nine of Owen's poems for the words in his moving *War Requiem*, a musical piece written for choir and orchestra. A requiem is a song of mourning for the dead, and Britten wrote his to honour the rebuilding of a cathedral that had been destroyed in World War II.

All Quiet on the Western Front paved the way for other authors to write about the war humanely and honestly. Also set during World War I, Humphrey Cobb's 1935 novel *Paths of Glory* deals with the French army's execution of soldiers for cowardice. Dalton Trumbo's *Johnny Got His Gun* (1939) is another anti-war novel about a young soldier who is wounded so badly that he cannot communicate with anyone.

German chancellor Helmut Kohl and French president François Mitterand hold hands at a World War II ceremony in 1984. Both countries suffered massive loss of life in the war.

NOVELS OF WORLD WAR II

In Catch-22, author Joseph Heller used a darkly comic tone to update many of Remarque's themes in the context of World War II. These include the abuse of power in the military, the insanity of combat, and the closeness of those who fight together. In Remarque's novel, Paul complains about how factory owners grow wealthy while the soldiers eating their food get sick. Heller goes a step further in attacking those who profit from war by having one character use military planes to sell goods all over the world, even to the enemy! Other important World War II novels that, like Remarque's work, deal with the struggle to be an individual in the military are The Naked and the Dead by Norman Mailer and From Here to Eternity by James Jones.

German reunification in 1990, 45 years after the end of World War II, was an important symbol of peace.

Lasting peace?

Remarque's work has continued to inspire those who work for peace. To acknowledge his lasting achievement, his hometown of Osnabrück, Germany, has been awarding the Erich Maria Remarque Peace Prize every other year since 1991. It honours men and women all over the world who help to end conflict, by building bridges of understanding.

There have been many important changes since Paul Bäumer's time. Most nations no longer celebrate the "glory of war" through propaganda. Many avoid using under age soldiers, and none are allowed to use poison gas. Sadly, however, soldiers at war still live in a lonely and frightening world that few who do not share it can understand. Perhaps *All Quiet on the Western Front* will always be popular because it can help readers to understand questions about war better. In a strange way, then, Remarque might have looked forward to the day when his book is no longer a best seller, because without wars, people will no longer need to ask such questions.

> **We have to believe in the future, in a better future. The world wants peace …**
>
> Erich Maria Remarque in a 1946 interview

TIMELINE

1888	Kaiser Wilhelm II becomes ruler of Germany.
1891–1905	Schlieffen, in charge of German military, develops his plan.
1898	Erich Maria Remarque is born in Osnabrück, Germany.
1914	World War I begins: France, Germany, and Britain declare war.
1915	Poison gas first used in battle.
1916	Battles of Verdun and the Somme are fought.
1917	Remarque joins German army and is wounded near Ypres, Belgium.
1917	United States declares war on Germany on 4 April.
1918	Armistice agreed to by warring countries on 11 November.
1919	Start of Germany's Weimar Republic government.
1919	28 June: Treaty of Versailles signed.
1920	Remarque publishes his first novel, *The Dream Room*.
1922	Fascist Mussolini takes power in Italy.
1923	Hitler imprisoned after trying to take power in Munich, Germany.
1923	French invasion of Germany's Ruhr region.
1924	Hitler's *Mein Kampf* (*My Struggle*) is published.
1925	*Mrs. Dalloway* by Virginia Woolf is published.
1925	Remarque marries Ilse Jutta (Jeanne) Zambona.
1926	*The Sun Also Rises* by Ernest Hemingway is published.
1927	Remarque writes *All Quiet on the Western Front*.
1928	*All Quiet on the Western Front* serialized.
1929	*All Quiet on the Western Front* published in Germany and other nations.
1930	Remarque divorces Jeanne Zambona.
1931	*All Quiet on the Western Front* named best US film of 1930.
1931	Remarque's *The Road Back*, the sequel to *All Quiet on the Western Front*, is published.
1933	Remarque flees Germany on 29 January.
1933	Hitler becomes German leader on 30 January.
1933	*All Quiet on the Western Front* copies destroyed in Nazi book burning on 10 May.

1936	Italy invades Ethiopia.
1939	World War II begins as Germany invades Poland.
1939–1945	The Holocaust: millions of Jews and other people are killed by the Nazis.
1945	World War II ends; Germany divided by victors.
1958	Remarque marries Paulette Goddard.
1961	*Catch-22* by Joseph Heller is published.
1962	Benjamin Britten's *War Requiem* premieres.
1970	Remarque dies.
1984	French and German leaders honour the dead of World War I.
1990	East and West Germany become one nation again.
1991	Erich Maria Remarque Peace Prize is awarded for the first time.

The edition used in the writing of this book is *All Quiet on the Western Front* (Lion Books, Inc NY, 1956 reprint of 1929 Little, Brown and Company edition).

Selected works by Erich Maria Remarque

The Road Back, 1931
Three Comrades, 1937
The Spark of Life, 1952
Time to Love and a Time to Die, 1954
The Black Obelisk, 1956

Books about World War I

Allan, Tony. *20th Century Perspectives: The Causes of World War I* (Heinemann Library, 2002)
Connolly, Sean. *Witness to History: World War I* (Heinemann Library, 2004)
Hibbert, Adam. *On the Front Line: In the Trenches in World War I* (Raintree, 2005)
Sheehan, Sean; Levy, Pat. *Modern Eras Uncovered: From the Wright Brothers to the Treaty of Versailles, The 1900s–1918* (Raintree, 2005)

World War I novels and poetry

Crane, Stephen. *The Red Badge of Courage and Other Stories* (Penguin Books, 2005)
Egremont, Max. *Siegfried Sassoon* (Picador, 2000)
Graves, Robert. *Goodbye to All That* (Penguin Books, 2000)
Heller, Joseph. *Catch 22* (Vintage, 2005)
Hemingway, Ernest. *The Sun Also Rises* (Arrow, 1994)
Jones, James. *From Here to Eternity* (Gramercy Books, 2004)
Remarque, Erich Maria. *All Quiet on the Western Front* (Vintage, 2005)
Sassoon, Seigfried. *Memoirs of an Infantry Officer* (Faber and Faber, 2000)
Sassoon, Seigfried. *The War Poems* (Faber and Faber, 2000)
Stallworthy, Jon. *The Faber Wilfred Owen* (Faber and Faber, 2000)
West, Rebecca. *Return of the Soldier* (Penguin Books, 1998)
Woolf, Virginia. *Mrs Dalloway* (Harvest Books, 2005)

Useful websites

www.hcu.ox.ac.uk/jtap
The Wilfred Owen Multimedia Digital Archive (WOMDA)
Users can browse through manuscripts, photographs, period film footage of the Western Front, and audio clips of interviews with World War I veterans.
www.Firstworldwar.com
From poetry to poison gas, from songs to propaganda posters, this amazing site has it all. An excellent resource, complete with vintage audio recordings.
www.nyu.edu/ library
Search for "Remarque". In 1990, Remarque's widow Paulette Goddard gave thousands of pages of personal documents and photos to the Fales Library at New York University.
www.remarque.uos.de
Erich Maria Remarque-Archive (also known as Research Center "War and Literature"). The archive provides a list of publications by and about Remarque.

Places to contact or visit

Memorial
The Cenotaph on London's Whitehall is the site of an annual service on Remembrance Sunday, (second Sunday in November, to be near Armistice Day annniversary). The Queen, members of the government and of the armed forces lay wreaths. The 1920 stone memorial's simple inscription reads "The glorious dead".

Museums and art exhibitions
Imperial War Museum
Lambeth Road, London SE1 6HZ
www.iwm.org.uk/
The museum also has an online gallery where you can search for paintings by war artists commissioned by the government to depict World War I.
Erich Maria Remarque-Exhibition
Markt 6, D-49069 Osnabrück, Germany
www.remarque.uos.de/internet.htm
Tate Modern, Bankside, London, SE1 9TG
The best place to see the work of war artist Paul Nash. The gallery has 30 works by him. See the online gallery at Tate Online www.tate.org./uk.
Legion of Honor Museum, San Francisco
www.thinker.org/legion/index.asp
Houses a large collection of paintings relating to WWI, as well as work by Otto Dix.

alliance association or partnership that benefits all involved

Allies/Allied Powers [in World War I] France, Britain, and Russia. President Woodrow Wilson did not want the United States to be considered an official part of this group; however, in World War II the term did include the United States

armistice agreement between two or more countries to stop fighting

atrocities unjustifiable acts of brutality or cruelty

Austria-Hungary an empire created in 1867 that, in addition to Austria and Hungary, included several other central European lands

battle plane fighter aircraft

camaraderie deep friendship between people living or working together

casualties those killed, wounded, or taken prisoner during war

Central Powers [in World War I] Germany, Austria-Hungary, the Ottoman Empire (Turkey), and Bulgaria

civilians people who are not in the armed forces

colony country or area under control of another country

comrade close friend with a common situation or interests

conscientious objector person who refuses to kill in combat, usually because of religious or moral beliefs

culture everything that expresses a group's traditional way of life

democracy form of government in which the people have power

deserter person in the army who leaves a group or post without permission

empire group of countries or states ruled by a single emperor

expressionism early 20th century style of art that stresses feelings over realistic images

fascism the idea that society can be remade through group strength and unity, a system in which individuals are not important

fortifications defences against attack such as walls and barriers

Front [Western or Eastern] line of contact between two opposing armies or forces

hampered held back

Holocaust period from 1939 until 1945 when Nazi Germany slaughtered millions of Jews and other people in Europe

hyperinflation monetary inflation that happens at a very fast rate

insincere not genuine

kaiser German word for emperor, based on the word Roman term "Caesar"

literary to do with literature

mobilize assemble, organize, or move into position

mustard gas named after its smell, this poison gas was made from several chemicals, including chlorine. First used in 1917, its use is now banned.

narrator character who tells a story

National Socialist Party fascist political party led by Adolf Hitler that controlled Germany from 1933 until 1945

Nazi member of the National Socialist Party

neutral not supporting either side in a conflict

No Man's Land region between the front lines of two opposing armies, often destroyed by fighting

observation plane military plane especially designed to observe or spy on the enemy

parapet low wall around a roof, bridge or other structure. In World War I: in front of the trench.

patriotism loyalty to, and affection for, your own country

post-traumatic stress disorder condition in which a terrible event causes lasting emotional harm

propaganda spreading of information and ideas to influence people's beliefs and actions

psychological related to the human mind

psychologists people who study the human mind

Reichstag name for the German parliament and also the name of the building in Berlin where the parliament met

reparations payments imposed on countries intended to make up for doing something wrong

review the troops inspect soldiers

serialized published in different parts over time

shells hollow metal containers filled with explosives or chemicals

shell shock psychological disturbance or trauma caused by being exposed to warfare

shrapnel pieces of flying metal that come from an explosive device

traumatic deeply distressing or upsetting

trench warfare type of fighting in which soldiers dig ditches into the ground facing each other

truce ceasefire or armistice between warring groups

U-boat shortened version of the German word *Unterseeboot*: a German submarine

under age below the legal age limit; in World War I under age soldiers usually meant those younger than eighteen

universal true for all people everywhere

veteran former member of the armed forces

Titles in the *History in Literature* series include:

Hardback   0 431 08137 3

Hardback   0 431 08170 0

Hardback   0 431 08169 7

Hardback   0 431 08173 5

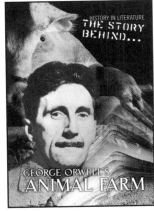

Hardback   0 431 08168 9

Hardback   0 431 08175 1

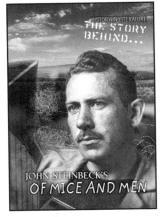

Hardback   0 431 08172 7

Hardback   0 431 08171 9

Find out about other titles from Heinemann Library on our website www.heinemann.co.uk/library